Growing Up in Pandupur

Adithi and Chatura Rao

Illustrations by
Krishna Bala Shenoi

SCHOLASTIC
New York Toronto London Auckland
Sydney New Delhi Hong Kong

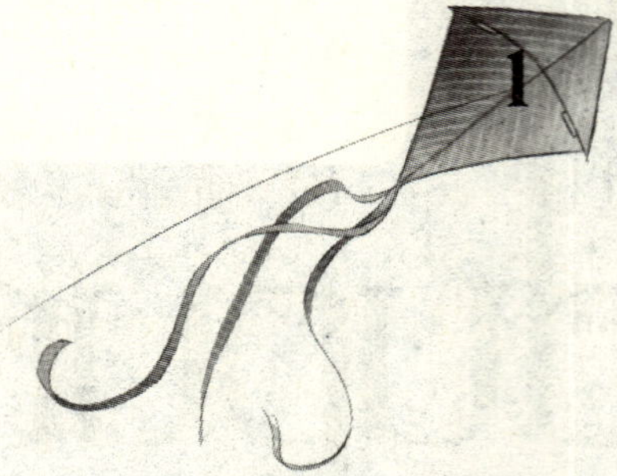

POLKA-DOTTED PARTY

Adithi Rao

'Ma, this year I'll have my birthday party at Pizza Stop,' said Raghav, strolling into the room, dragging his skates behind him by their laces. His mother was helping Tara with her homework.

'We'll talk about it later,' she muttered, her eyes on the Maths sum she was tackling.

'*Ma-aa*,' persisted Raghav, 'this can't wait, okay? My birthday is only a month away. I'm telling you, Pizza Stop is where I want it.'

'Tara, when you take the denominator to the ...'

'MA!' yelled Raghav, making his mother and sister jump.

'*What*!' demanded his mother, spinning around in her chair and glowering at him.

'I said, my party ...'

'We heard you, Raag Bhaiyya,' eleven-year-old Tara cut in with an air of great seriousness. 'Oh, and ma, don't forget to write *Happy Birthday to* "*Rags*" on the cake. Raghav is too uncool.

GROWING UP IN PANDUPUR

Adithi graduated from Smith College, USA, with a degree in Theatre, and returned to India to work as an assistant director on the Hindi film *Satya*. *Shakuntala & Other Timeless Tales of Ancient India* is her first book for children. *Growing up in Pandupur* is her second. When the Muse comes knocking, Adithi pens the occasional film script, the rights to one of which was bought by Aamir Khan Productions Ltd. Over the years, her stories have appeared in children's anthology collections published by Penguin, Scholastic, Puffin and Zubaan. Her adult short fiction has been featured online, as well as in the print editions of *Longshot Island*, an American journal. In her free time, Adithi takes long walks and cooks food that her family politely enjoys.

Chatura's first book was a children's fantasy novel called *The Case of Disappearing Colour* (Puffin, 2004/Scholastic, 2013). Two picture books—*Nabiya* (Tulika, 2013) and *Gone Grandmother* (Tulika, 2016)—and *Growing Up in Pandupur* are her other books for children. Her first novel for adults was *Meanwhile Upriver* (Penguin, 2008). Her second, *A Blueprint for Love* (Bloomsbury), released in October 2016. Chatura is also an award-winning freelance journalist. She conducts creative writing workshops at Prithvi Theatre, Mumbai, and was curator of the Chandigarh Children's Literature Festival, 2016.

For mothers,
Vimala, Sudha, Sheila, Bharati
and daughters,
Pratyangira, Achala, Nandini

This book is an abridged version of *Growing Up In Pandupur* (Scholastic India, 2017)

Published by Scholastic India Pvt. Ltd.
A subsidiary of Scholastic Inc., New York, 10012 (USA).
Publishers since 1920, with international operations in Canada, Australia, New Zealand, the United Kingdom, India, and Hong Kong.

For information regarding permission, write to:
Scholastic India Pvt. Ltd.
A-27, Ground Floor, Sigma Centre
Infocity-1, Sector 34, Gurgaon 122001 (India)

First original edition: June 2017
This edition: April 2018

ISBN: 978-93-5275-452-6

Printed at Shivam Offset Press, New Delhi

He'll get kicked out of his gang if any of them is reminded of his real name.'

Sheila, their mother, was laughing now. But Raghav was furious. He stomped out of the room. The expensive pair of skates bumped and scraped their way down the back porch stairs. Papa had bought them for Raghav the last time he had gone to the big city to meet with the chief engineer on the Dhun River Dam project.

As site engineer, Raghav and Tara's father had to make frequent trips to the head office in the city, and Raghav always expected a gift at the end of each trip. Well, it was the price Papa had to pay for relocating his whole family from their bustling home city to the placid township of Pandupur. Sheila and Tara seemed to like it here though ...

Plans were underway for Raghav's party. The cake had been ordered (chocolate butter, shaped like a Power Ranger), the party floor of the Pizza Stop had been booked, and invitation cards printed. There were ten days left for the party ... nine ... eight ... seven ... when a bright pink spot appeared on Raghav's chest. Another one appeared on his arm, a third on his cheek and a fourth on his nose ...

'Chicken pox!' pronounced the doctor. 'Has Tara had it?'

Sheila nodded.

'She's safe then,' said Dr Bhaskara. 'Well, Raghav, no school for a while! That should be good news for you.'

'For how long, doctor?' asked Sheila.

'Hard to say. It could go on for a week ... maybe longer.'

'Longer?!' exclaimed Raghav. 'But my party is coming up. There's no way I'm going to miss that!'

The next week was terrible. Everybody in school heard

about Raghav's chicken pox. By the end of the week, Sheila had received phone calls from the mothers of Raghav's friends, declining the invitation to his birthday party. The excuses were varied but ingenious.

'Sunil is going to visit his grandmother that day.' (That Sunil's grandmother lived in the mountains with sixteen dogs was common knowledge.)

'Er … are Nitin and Raghav even that close?' (Everybody knew that if Raghav jumped from the 15th floor without a parachute, Nitin would jump off behind him.)

'Our astrologer has told us not to leave the house for all of next week.'

'Thanks, but no thanks!'

And finally …

'Zayan has had the chicken pox already, so he'll definitely attend the party!'

The party was cancelled.

***

On the morning of his birthday, Raghav stepped out of the shower with his Pokémon towel wrapped around his waist. As he examined himself in the foggy bathroom mirror, he saw that the scabs on his chicken pox sores had fallen off, but he still had spots on his face. Two, three … six in all. Great! Now he could be the ugly birthday boy at the party he wasn't going to have! At least he hoped his mother had taken the hint and reminded Papa to buy him that Play Station. Raghav hated being stuck here in Pandupur, far away from the city that was his home, from the malls and his friends at Haley's International School. The Pizza Stop, indeed! Not Hut, *Stop*. This is how down-market his life had become!

When Raghav came down for breakfast, Tara cried, 'Happy

Birthday, Bhaiyya!' and gave him a bear hug. He pretended to fend her off because it was not cool to hug one's little sister. Sheila whisked out a basket of brightly wrapped gifts from under the table. Raghav's heart leapt and he dived in with gusto. He ripped open the first packet and pulled out …

'Red and blue socks! What the heck for?'

'To match your blue-and-red-flag underwear.'

'I don't have blue-and-red-flag underwear,' said Raghav in disgust.

'You do now!' grinned Tara, pulling out a pair from another wrapper and waving it at her brother. Raghav's next present was a book.

'*Doggie Advice for Idiots*,' he read from the cover. 'What nonsense is this! I don't even *have* a dog … What the …!'

Something was licking his ankles! Raghav squeaked and leapt backwards, looking down. Then he froze, somewhere between disbelief and ... sheer delight! There was a puppy at his feet! A little black creature with a white spot on its fuzzy forehead.

Raghav dropped to his knees and swept the puppy up into his arms. The little thing wriggled and squirmed, licking him all over his face.

'Hey, Ma! Think he'll be upset we didn't get the Play Station?' laughed Tara.

Raghav glanced up quickly. His eyes met his mother's. He smiled and shook his head.

A little later, when Raghav and Archie the puppy were up in their room doing homework (which meant that Archie was chewing up a Maths worksheet and Raghav was watching in admiration), Raghav noticed a bright blue envelope on his dresser. It was the same invite that had been printed for his Pizza Stop party, only this one was addressed to him in Tara's handwriting.

Dear Raghav & Archie,

Do join me, Rags, in celebrating my 13th birthday.

Venue: ~~Pizza Stop~~ The Little Pandavas Orphanage, Pandupur

Time: 5 pm

Date: 5th August

Dress Code: Shabby!

Don't miss it, or you'll be sorrrrrryyyy!

This sounded far, far worse than chicken pox and no party at all!

'Ma,' grumbled Raghav, flouncing into the kitchen, 'no way am I going to some stupid party at an *orphanage*!'

'Of course you are,' replied his mother cheerfully.

At 4.30 that evening, Raghav was dressed in shabby clothes and an equally shabby expression. Archie was sporting a bow tie and tearing around the garden like a mad thing. Sheila came out dressed in simple clothes.

'Tara's gone ahead, so it's just us two ... three,' she corrected, when she saw Archie. 'Shall we?'

The Little Pandavas Orphanage was in Chikku Colony, close to the tribal settlement on the edge of the forest. The place was simple but neat, painted in bright colours and surrounded by the greenery of the woodland beyond. When they reached the orphanage, they found Tara and all the "Little Pandavas" waiting for them in a solemn group at the gate. They had pink spots painted all over their faces! Raghav stared in astonishment.

'Are you making fun of me?' he squeaked.

'We didn't want you to feel out of place,' said Tara, and held up a mirror to his face.

The spots on the others' faces were exactly like the ones on his! Raghav was about to laugh out loud, but he stopped himself. Instead, he scowled at one cheeky-looking youth and mumbled, 'You look stupid.'

'You too,' returned the boy politely.

'Games!' shouted Tara.

And all the poised, well-behaved orphans let out a yell and broke ranks. They went tearing around the back of the neat red-and-white building with Archie at their heels. The backyard was full of trees and had lots of place to run and play in.

'Okay, guys, now listen up!' bawled Tara. 'Our first game is lagori.'

'What's that?' asked Raghav.

The boy he had spoken to earlier—Prashant—explained. 'There are two teams. Seven flat stones piled one on top of the other. Team One has to fall down the stones with tennis ball. Then have to try to pile stones up again while Team Two tries to hit them with ball. If ball touches any of them before they manage to put up all seven stones, the whole team out. Otherwise it is "lagori!" for Team One and they win!'

'His English is pretty good,' said a surprised Raghav to Tara in an undertone, for he had been expecting them to speak only the local language.

'They study in Saraswati High School, Bhaiyya,' whispered Tara.

'They go to *school*?' asked Raghav, his eyebrows going up.

'Of course. Why are you so surprised?'

The game was a riot! Raghav's team knocked down the stones and then scattered in all directions, trying to get away from the ball. But every time the ball was thrown, Archie would pounce on it and carry it straight to Raghav.

'But you're on *our* team!' protested Ravi loudly to the dog. Archie looked unrepentant. Prashant, who was also on Ravi's team, gazed thoughtfully at Archie for a moment. Suddenly he grinned and whispered something in Ravi's ear. Ravi's face broke into a broad smile. 'S'alright!' he said and walked away with a spring in his step.

The next time Archie grabbed the ball and headed straight for Raghav, a hush fell over her team. They watched in expectant silence. Raghav grinned, bent down, and took the ball out of her mouth.

'Yay!' roared Archie's team.

'Out! Out!'

'What?' asked Raghav, looking around in confusion, the ball still in his hand.

'The ball is touching your body before you have put back the stones. You're out. Your whole team is out!' cried Prashant gleefully.

Realisation dawned on Raghav. He dropped the ball quickly, but it was too late. They had him! His teammates let out a yell of indignation. They lifted Raghav off his feet and chucked him into a mud puddle where he landed with a mighty splash.

'AAARGH!' Raghav felt cold clods of red mud slip under his shirt collar and down his back. Struggling up, he reached out and grabbed the nearest boy, pulling him down into the dirt with him. Before long, the lot of them were in the throes of a mud fight. Archie watched them with her head to one side. When Ravi slyly flung a handful of muck at her, her ears shot up into the air. With a yelp and a flying leap, she dived in with the rest, head first.

'Okay, time to cut the cake,' came Sheila's voice.

The fight broke up as quickly as it had begun. Many pairs of white eyes looked out of red muddy faces. Suddenly they burst out laughing, holding on to each other. Raghav was laughing with the rest of them, and he was having the time of his life.

They washed up noisily in the water tank, then made their way to the rickety table on which the Power Ranger cake was laid out.

'Happy Birthday Rags,' one little boy read off the cake. '"*Rags?*"' he repeated, looking puzzled. 'Why you are calling yourself "old clothes"?'

Raghav blushed scarlet. He had never thought of it that way before.

The children burst into the birthday song. Then they attacked the cake, chips, sandwiches and samosas until all the food was gone. When it was time to leave, Raghav and Tara shook hands all around.

'Thanks,' said Raghav awkwardly to Prashant, but his eyes were shining.

Prashant nodded cordially. 'Come again. You are not so bad.'

Raghav grinned. Somehow it was hard to take offence to that.

Later that night, as Tara was stepping into her room, Raghav caught up with her in the corridor and hugged her quickly.

'That was the best polka-dotted birthday party I've ever had,' he mumbled, then disappeared into his room and shut the door. Out in the corridor, Tara's face lit up with a smile.

'You're welcome, Raag Bhaiyya,' she said, to nobody at all.

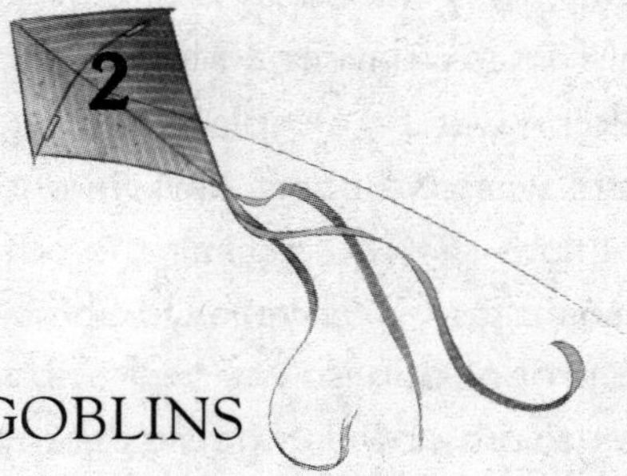

2

GOBLINS

Chatura Rao

This gang believed in goblin power. Know what goblins are? They are small, powerful, malevolent fairy-beings who roam about in bands. They live in dark underground places, overpowering other fairy folk and making them work as slaves.

Tejas, who was twelve years old, had just read *The Hobbit*. He wanted to be a goblin, so he formed this band with his friends. They called themselves Hobgobs One, meaning that they thought as one, and acted as one. The members of Hobgobs One were Pratik, Akshat, Vistasp and Tejas himself, who was Hobgob Supreme, the twisted leader.

So far, the Hobgobs had contented themselves with small acts of mischief in and around Postal Colony, which adjoined the Pandupur Market. They had painted red spots on the white roses on Mr Patil's bushes, and left him a note saying that the roses had measles and he should call a doctor. One Sunday morning they'd sprinkled water on the fresh newspapers lying on people's doormats. They had rung old Shakira Aunty's doorbell (and run away) six times a day for a week, making her wail with anger, until the building watchman spied them out.

There was one other person who wanted to be a Hobgob. She was sure she could make the outfit more evil than it already was: Tejas' sister, nine-year-old Shivi. But Tejas had told her that to be a proper goblin, you had to be a boy. Shivi did not agree. Girls can also be cruel and turn other people into slaves, she said. Look at Amma!

Indeed, their mother was very strict. If a crust of bread was left behind in their tiffin box when they returned from school, she would box their ears. If the bed was not made neatly, there would be a pinch on the back of their palms. If there were careless mistakes in their classwork, there would be a rap on the knuckles. Why was Amma so stern? The children's father did not live with them, so perhaps Amma wanted to make no mistakes in bringing them up. She got really tired everyday, what with her day job at the post office, tuitions in the evenings, and Shivi and Tejas to take care of.

However, at night, before they slept, Amma would sit with her legs folded into her flowing kaftan and her soft hair let down, as the children lay in bed and told her how their day had been. At bedtime, all mistakes were forgiven and anger shed. Amma would pretend to roll the problems of the day into a ball. She rolled them nice and tight and then flung them out of the open window, far into outer space, so that the children would sleep well and dream easy.

One Sunday the neighbours complained about being hit by water balloons from their balcony. So Amma grounded Shivi and Tejas. 'We are like silly Hansel and Gretel, stuck in this house with the wicked witch,' Shivi grumbled.

'*You* can be silly sometimes, Gretel,' Tejas sneered. 'But *I* am the Hobgob Supreme!'

'Like Chocolate Supreme from the Pandu Ice Cream Parlour?' Shivi giggled.

'Shut up, you dwarf!' the goblin said, pushing her down. He turned away, rubbing his red ears that had recently been boxed by Amma. Peering into the dressing table mirror, he practiced an evil smile. His sister was sitting on the floor, controlling her tears, but he ignored her.

He turned his head from side to side. His ears actually seemed to be growing sharp and big like real goblin ears. So what if they still stung? He would get his goblin gang together and do something really mean. Tomorrow when this punishment ended, he and the gang would find and train their first slave.

The next evening the Hobgobs pinpointed their victim, Neville, a boy from their building who lived on the first floor. Neville was short for a ten-year-old, a bit squat with a flat nose and small eyes. He wore the same set of clothes every day—blue T-shirt and dark brown pants. He did not have the trendy sunglasses, football or bicycle that the other boys had. He was alone a lot.

Sometimes Shivi played with him because they had gone to the same neighbourhood nursery school when they were three years old. Also, they both liked reading. A few times Neville had helped her with her homework. He studied a lot, because, as he told her, he wanted to grow up and get a well-paying job. As for Shivi, she didn't bother much about studying or growing up. She mostly tagged behind her brother and his gang.

'Want to be in our gang?' Tejas asked Neville that evening by the stairs, where he was playing with an old-fashioned top. Tejas winked slyly at Pratik. Vistasp and Akshat had already started snickering.

'Me? Why?' Neville stammered, surprised that Tejas was even talking to him.

'Because you have brains,' Tejas replied. 'The Hobgobs have strength. You'd be a fundoo addition to our gang.'

Neville was convinced. Shivi watched from a distance as her brother and his friends huddled in a knot with Neville in the centre. They were teaching him the secret password, which he swore he would never disclose to anybody, not even if subjected to interrogation. Shivi frowned, wondering why they were initiating Neville into their gang. He was a head shorter than the rest, and very uncool. The only thing he had going for him was that he was a boy (if goblins *had* to be boys).

'We'll need to train you. "Fitness is Fundoo" is one of the mottos of this gang. Report at the building lobby tomorrow at three in the afternoon,' Vistasp instructed him. That was homework time, but Neville smiled and nodded, his little eyes shining.

The next day, at 3 p.m., the four boys followed by Shivi entered the lobby, having just got off the school bus. They found Neville waiting.

Tejas gave Neville the special Hobgob handshake. The rest did the same. Neville felt proud despite his shortness and his old blue shirt and faded brown pants. 'What should I do now?' he asked them.

'Now,' Pratik said very seriously, 'weight training for you. Carry our school bags up to our houses. Then come and wait here by the stairs till we change our clothes and come back downstairs ...'

'No,' Tejas said with authority, a finger to his forehead. 'Why waste time waiting? Take my bag and run around the building three times, as a workout. Then open the bag and ... do my Maths homework.'

'W ... why?' Neville asked uncertainly.

'Why? *Why*?!' Akshat exclaimed. 'Are you a Hobgob or not? We Hobgobs think as one. We ask no questions!' They leaned forward, closing in on him. Shivi, who had been finishing her packed lunch in a corner, sensed trouble and looked up.

'It's okay, boys,' Tejas said, waving them back. 'He's new and he doesn't know how we operate. Look here, Neville, in order to be a part of us, you have to learn to obey gang instructions without question. That is why you will be made to do some unusual tasks. My Maths homework is just one of them. You may be asked to polish shoes sometimes. But when you're fully trained to obey and think like us, you will have equal rights in the gang. Alright?'

That afternoon Neville carried bags, ran around the building, and did everybody's Maths homework.

In the evening, when Shivi came down to play, she found Neville sitting in a corner, polishing Tejas' leather belt. The sight of him hunched over it brought on a rush of anger. She knew the Hobgobs' secret aim to make slaves out of other people. And although she had wanted to be a cruel Hobgob herself, she didn't like seeing Neville this way. He was her friend.

'Neville, don't polish Tejas' belt! He's just bullying you.'

'It's not bullying,' Neville shrugged. 'I don't mind. I polish my Papa's shoes, so I'm used to polishing. Besides, it's my last training task of the day. Tomorrow I *may* get to be an equal member of the Hobgobs ...'

Shivi knew it was no use reasoning with him. She could see a sort of slavish look settling into his eyes already. She raced over to where her brother and his gang were playing football.

'How dare you make Neville polish your belt? Are you a prince or something to make people your slaves?' she shouted.

Tejas glared at her in anger. He really felt like slapping her, but his mother would punish them severely if they had a fist fight in public. They did not notice that Neville had stopped shining the belt and was watching intently from where he sat.

'Hey, it's just Shivi,' Pratik said nastily, coming to stand beside Tejas. 'Curious Shivi with a big nose come to spy! Come closer, Nosey, I'll give you something to smell.' He wiggled his behind at her. The rest laughed, Tejas pretending to join them. Shivi did have a rather large nose, but Pratik's was even bigger.

'You're a Gang of One!' Shivi cried. 'Four bodies, one brain! Oh, sorry. No brain. I was mistaking Neville for one of you, so I counted his.'

Pratik reached out and twisted Shivi's pigtail. He held on, even when she screamed. Now Shivi was used to her mother boxing her ears, but this was different. She felt angry and humiliated. 'Anna!' she cried out to her older brother as she tried to squirm out of Pratik's grasp. But Tejas stood there, confused. Shivi was his sister but she had insulted him in front of his friends. Besides, the Hobgobs had promised to stand as One, so he had to back Pratik.

Suddenly something bashed into Pratik from behind. He stumbled forward, letting go of Shivi's hair. Vistasp, Akshat and Tejas grabbed Neville's arms to prevent him from running at Pratik again. 'You leave her alone!' Neville shouted. He tried to kick Pratik again, which is when the other three boys held him down. All this didn't last long, as two women and the building watchman came over and broke up the group and prevented the thrashing that Neville would surely have got at this point.

When Amma came home, Shivi did not complain to her about the incident. She had never reported Tejas' behaviour, no matter what he did to her. *She's brave for a girl*, Tejas admitted reluctantly to himself.

But Shivi had written him a note and left it on his desk:

'You think you are a hero. But you are a coward and a bully. Today you did not help me, which means that Pratik and your gang are more important to you than I am. Neville may be short and not very strong, but he is still ten times braver than you.'

Tejas had known that he would eventually have made Pratik let go of Shivi's hair. But the few seconds of hesitation had cost him her respect. Somehow that made him feel bad inside. He should have stood up for his sister.

'And what about Neville?' a voice inside him asked. Neville did not have anyone to stand up for him. No big brother or anybody. Tejas felt uneasy.

At bedtime, when Amma came to sit with them, she found the children pretending to be asleep. Smiling to herself, she prayed over them, kissed their foreheads and went away.

The next evening, at playtime, Tejas spoke very little to the other Hobgobs. Instead, he went up to Neville who was bouncing and catching a rubber ball alone by the stairs.

'Hi, Neville,' Tejas said.

'I don't want to join your gang,' Neville said, turning away.

'I don't care about that,' Tejas said to Neville's back. 'I just wanted to talk about yesterday ... er ... that is, I wanted to ask if you want to come play cricket?'

Even as Neville looked around in surprise, Tejas felt his little sister's hand slip into his and squeeze it. He looked down at her

standing by his side, a happy smile below her big nose and shining brown eyes. The company of dwarves might be a little boring, Tejas shrugged, but what the heck! It wasn't so bad either.

So the ex-Hobgob Supreme smiled at the two by his side and they walked together towards the playground.

3

CHANGING CHINTAMANI

Adithi Rao

Daadi disapproved. She was not particular about what. She just needed something to disapprove of to make her day. There are millions of grandmothers in the world, so you might be wondering which one I'm talking about. Let me be specific. This is Chintamani's daadi. His father's mother.

Chintamani? Is that his name? Sure. Daadi chose it. His mother wanted to call him Chetan, but his grandmother put her foot down, and now there is a twelve-year-old person living in New Society, Pandupur, walking about with the name Chintamani. I won't even go into all the teasing and name-calling the poor kid puts up with on a daily—no, make that hourly—basis!

Chintamani's mother, Mrs Nandini Bahadur, was a quiet woman, never speaking much. Usually it was Daadi who did the talking. Her word was the law in the house, and Chintamani's

Papa, who thought highly of his mother, allowed his household to be governed by this She-Man.

Chintamani wasn't particularly good at anything—neither studies nor sports nor the usual extracurricular activities that other boys of his age are usually good at. He didn't even catch the brightly coloured lizards that strayed into people's yards from the surrounding forest, collect beetles or bully puppies like the other boys did.

Our story begins on the day he came home with a Report Card. A Report Card and a Request. The Report Card showed that he had failed in Maths and Science. The Request was worded like this: 'Papa, can I go for a football training camp this summer?'

'No, you may not!' replied Daadi bossily, before her son could speak.

Even Chintamani's mother looked up, a little surprised at how her son could make such a request within minutes of presenting his execrable exam results. From her corner of the room she searched the child's face. His eyes were clear as ever. That's what his mother loved most about him—his calm, innocent eyes. She went back to cutting vegetables, but she kept a keen ear on the conversation.

'Please? I want to learn football,' ventured the boy.

'Are you mad!' exclaimed his father. 'After scoring such low marks?'

'First pass your exams. No need for distractions!' Thus Daadi put an end to the conversation. Chintamani went away quietly.

'Why do you want football coaching, Chintu?' asked his mother that night, as she smoothed down the cover of his warm Jaipuri quilt.

His sleepy round face became awake at the question. 'So I can be good at it, Ma. I like it, but I'm bad at it.'

His mother looked at him in silence for a moment. Then she nodded and sighed.

In bed that night, she raised the subject with her husband a little nervously. 'Maybe Chintu can go for coaching? It's during the summer holidays and …'

'He's terrible at basketball,' said her husband dismissively.

'But he wants to learn *football*.'

'Oh. Well, he'll be terrible at that too.'

Chintamani's mother frowned a little. 'How can we know that before he's even had a chance to try?'

'He's bad at everything. Or haven't you noticed?'

'He hasn't tried everything …' she tried to reason, but her husband flared up.

'Did you see his marks, Nandini? And what about basketball? I tried playing with him the other day but he was just … so … my God, I was mortified! Everybody was laughing at him. And at me for trying to teach him.'

That night there was no sleep for Chintamani's mother. She tossed and turned in bed, until, towards the early hours of the morning, her troubled thoughts finally gave way to a plan …

***

A nagging sound penetrated Chintamani's slumbering brain. It grew higher and louder until it became a wail. Jolted awake, he shot up in bed, thinking, 'A cat is dying!' But then he slumped back down, shaking his head. It was just Daadi singing. Today was Friday then. Every Friday she sang bhajans.

Twenty minutes later, Chintamani went downstairs in his uniform, looking funny as usual. His wet hair was parted in the centre and flattened on either side of his head. He hated it. It made him look like a talking monkey from the *Panchatantra Tales*. But what could he do? That's how his grandmother insisted he comb his hair.

As he sat at the breakfast table, he noticed his mother was dressed to go out.

'Where are you going?' demanded the grandmother, sauntering out of the prayer room.

'To speak to Chintamani's teachers about Maths coaching in the summer holidays, Ammaji,' replied Nandini. The paratha turned to sawdust in Chintamani's mouth. Extra classes!

As they walked down to school together, Ma looked different somehow. There was a grim determination about her face that he had never seen there before. Used to her soft-voiced requests, he was taken aback when she fished a comb out of her purse and said briskly, 'Let's change that hairstyle, shall we?'

They reached the tall gates of Stone Valley International School. Chintamani grew nervous at the prospect of his mother meeting his teachers. What terrible things would they tell her about him? But instead of walking in the direction of the school building, his mother strode off towards the playground.

'Ma! Where're you going? It's this way.'

She shook her head and kept walking, and Chintamani, confused, trailed after her. She went to the vast school playground, where the coach was training some boys at football. He was strict and rigorous, and didn't spare them, but he seemed to be very good at his job. After watching the man quietly for a few minutes, Chintamani's mother walked up to him. Chintamani broke out into a cold sweat.

'I would like to sign up my son for the football coaching camp this summer.'

Chintamani's jaw dropped open. The coach shot the boy a

quick, appraising look and then came to rest on the face of the determined lady before him.

'Chintamani has never liked sports much,' he said curtly.

'It is his wish to learn.' Her voice was neutral.

'This camp is not just a way to pass the time during the vacations, madam. It is intended to rigorously train my boys at the sport. By the end of it we will have selections for the school team. We compete against the top teams of schools from Bangalore and Mysore. It won't be easy at all. And to be honest, your son knows nothing about the game ...'

'I was watching you just now, Sir. I'm sure you're more than up to teaching him.'

The coach paused for a moment, considering her words. 'Okay, if that is how you feel, you can sign him up. It will cost five thousand rupees for six weeks.' Chintamani's eyes flew to his mother's face. He knew that was a lot of money for her to arrange without his father knowing it. But she only nodded.

At dinner, Chintamani's father said, 'Ammaji says you are arranging for extra Maths class for Chintamani.'

'Yes. Five days a week for six weeks.'

Chintamani expected her to keep her eyes on her plate as she told this lie, but he was surprised. She looked directly at her husband.

The summer holidays began. Chintamani's mother got out his next year's text books and made him study, teaching him for hours each morning. Then she packed a bag with a set of sports clothes and running shoes. She made it a point to go with Chintamani to the football field every day. After each session she made him change back into his clean clothes so that he would look like he had been at the Maths class.

Once they reached the football ground, she sat in the stands, watching the session closely along with Raghav's mother, Sheila. As Nandini Bahadur observed the training, she started to understand why the coach had been reluctant to let Chintamani join the camp. The boy was awkward in his game. He was unconfident, whereas all the other boys were energetic and whole-hearted.

'What the hell are you doing?' yelled the coach suddenly at Chintamani, when the boy made an awkward pass.

'Looking Hong Kong, going Tokyo!' cackled Tejas.

Chintamani froze. His eyes went to his mother up in the stands. Her face remained expressionless. Finding no sympathy from that quarter, Chintamani turned red and mumbled an apology.

'You can't even pass straight. You'll have to work on your aim!' snapped the coach. Chintamani went redder still.

That evening, Chintamani went into the back garden. He stood beneath the rosewood tree, looking up into the branches. His father complained about Pandupur all the time, but Chintamani liked it here. It was quieter than Delhi, where they had lived before Papa got the job of working on the dam project. The people here were nice, and his best friend at Stone Valley had even taught him some words in the local language. *Ba* meant "come" and *illi* meant "here". The coach was always shouting '*Illi ba*!' to the boys during training. 'Come here!'

Stone Valley International was where the engineers' kids studied. Most of the junior officers sent their children to Saraswati Vidyashala along with the locals, because it didn't cost so much to go there. But some kids like Tejas who studied at Saraswati Vidyashala, were allowed to train at Stone Valley because they played extremely well. The coach had arranged it for them.

Chintamani took some green chalk out of his pocket and

drew a large circle on the garden wall. Then he placed his football on the ground some distance away and kicked it, aiming for the centre of the circle. He was way off. He kicked and kicked and missed and missed till he was tired and dejected. His mother, who was watching him from the kitchen window as she cooked, called out cheerfully, 'Don't give up! Keep trying!'

Back he went again. In the next fifty kicks, he managed to get the ball on target eight times.

The next day, the coach made the boys run the circumference of the field twice. Halfway into the first round, Chintamani began to tire. Raghav, who was alongside him, panted, 'Stop, and the coach will kick you right out of the training!'

Chintamani drew on his reserve strength and made one last great effort. Knowing his mother was watching made him want to try to keep going. As he ran, suddenly it got easier. He had got his second wind! Now he no longer ran to please his mother or the coach. He ran for the pure joy of feeling the wind in his face. He surged ahead of the others.

At the end of the second round, the boys came puffing up to stand before the coach.

'Take your positions!' called the coach curtly.

The boys dispersed to various parts of the field. 'You, Chintamani.'

Chintamani turned. 'You're a good runner,' said the coach. Then he blew the whistle to indicate the start of the game.

The next few weeks went by in a blur of studying, football training in school and practicing alone at home in the evenings. Out of every 100 kicks, 90 now zoomed straight to the centre of the chalk circle on the garden wall. Chintamani found that he could get the ball in from any angle, any distance away.

One day he came downstairs with his hair combed straight back and no centre parting.

'Going for some film shooting?' inquired his grandmother sarcastically when she saw him.

'No, Daadi, Maths class. But I still have to take pity on my teacher, or he'll go blind from looking at my terrible hairstyle day in and day out!' He gave his furious grandmother a quick hug and darted out of the house before she could slap him for his impertinence.

Out on the field that day, Chintamani played well. He ran like the wind, and his passes were clean and precise. Twice his teammates slapped him on the back approvingly, and once the coach called, '*Sakkath*!' which meant "terrific!"

The six weeks of coaching camp came to an end. Chintamani was miles ahead at football now than when he had started out. But then, so were all the others. Tryouts for the school team were in four days, and the competition was stiff.

On the morning of the tryouts, Chintamani's mother came to him in his room. She sat on the edge of his bed and said in her quiet way, 'Play with all your heart today. Don't worry about being selected.'

'But don't you want me to be on the team? Isn't that why you lied to Papa and Daadi to get me into coaching camp?' asked Chintamani, puzzled.

'No. I put you in that camp to show you that you can be good at anything you work at. Don't you think you are good at football now?'

'Yes,' said Chintamani, smiling.

'Then it was worth it.'

At 5 o'clock that evening, Chintamani was tearing down the

midfield, looking for someone to pass the ball to. Aryan, a right-winger, was nearby. Chintamani kicked the ball straight to him, a fraction of a second before an opponent shot a foot out to tackle Chintamani. That's when Chintamani's eyes fell on the stands ...

His father was there, sitting next to his mother! He was watching the game carefully, excitedly. But who was that little bundle wrapped in a bubblegum pink shawl perched on the other side of his father? In all of Pandupur, there must be only one woman who possessed a garment of that hair-raising shade—his grandmother! There she was, his grumpy Daadi, prayer beads in hand, probably praying for her recalcitrant grandson's soul!

'HAVE YOU LOST YOUR MIND, CHINTAMANI?' The coach's voice came clear at him from across the field. Jolted back to

reality, Chintamani tore off towards the goal.

Ten minutes later, the boys came off the field. They were tired, panting, a little tense. The coach stood there with a list in his hand. As Chintamani walked past him, the coach grumbled in a low voice, 'Daydreaming in the middle of the game! It almost cost you a place on the school team.'

Almost. Almost? *Almost*!

But not quite!

Chintamani stopped in his tracks as the words sank in. He spun around to look at his mother up in the stands and gave her his widest, happiest smile!

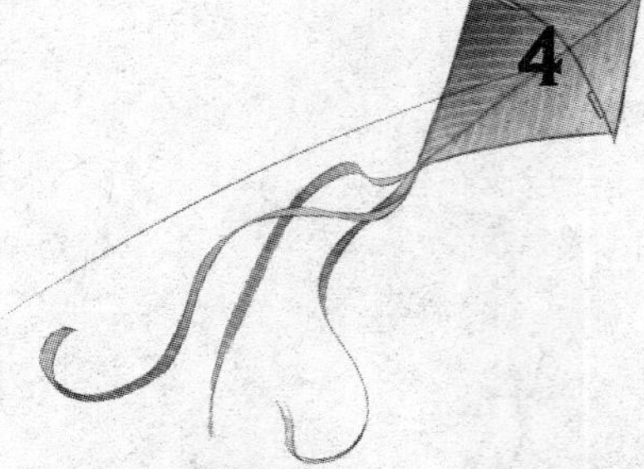

4

THE HOUSE PAINTED BLUE

Chatura Rao

Thangi and her best friends, the twins Situ and Gitu, lived in Chikku Colony. Many retired army people from other parts of the country lived in their neighbourhood. But mostly, the people who worked for the government forest department lived here, because Chikku Colony was on the edge of the Pandupur Nature Reserve. Occasionally a panther strayed into the tiny lanes of the colony, so no one let their children or pets play outside after sunset. But even the threat of wild animals was not exciting anymore. Everybody was used to it. Chikku Colony was a quiet place.

So this winter vacation, when things got a little too quiet, Thangi, Situ and Gitu began to watch the other houses really closely. The fun and fizz had to be hiding somewhere ... Maybe it was squeezed into somebody's fridge! Thangi and her friends were thirsty for it.

At first it was boring to keep watch. All the houses in Chikku

Colony were rectangular and cream-coloured, with brown edging. They had been built by the Housing Board to look exactly the same. Then Gitu pointed out that House No. 37, six plots away, had a hint of blue paint on its walls.

'How come?' Situ wondered. Thangi decided to ask her father.

'House No. 37 looked very different when I was a boy,' Appa told her at the dining table. 'It was painted sky blue, with curly white clouds floating just below the roof. Its owner used to live in Kashmir. Pass the rice, please.'

The owner of No. 37 must have missed that sky across which clouds rush and curl, Thangi decided, so he'd painted his house the same shade of blue. It certainly was different from the other coffee-and-cream houses in Chikku Colony. She tried to imagine house No. 37 when it was first painted like the mountain sky. When she closed her eyes, it looked very beautiful. But when she opened them, she saw that the blue paint had peeled off the walls and ugly brown patches were in its place. The clouds now looked like bubblegum that the roof had spat out.

The house belonged to an old air force pilot. People called him Hero Shambo. 'He won medals in two wars!' Situ's mother exclaimed.

But Thangi and Situ-Gitu knew that Colonel Shambo was a strange sort of hero. They hid behind the banyan tree across the street and peeked at his peeling house. This was what they saw.

Every day, Blackie the stray dog would go and sit by the gate of No. 37. Skinny old Colonel Shambo, wearing a pair of wireless headphones, would sneak out from behind the house. He'd fall to the ground and crawl through the uncut grass, all the time talking into his headphones. When Blackie whined with greed, the old man would sit up and dig in his pockets. He'd feed Blackie bread and biscuits, and pet him while he ate.

Then Colonel Shambo would do a funny thing. Real funny for a grown-up. The girls giggled, covering their mouths with their hands. He'd hobble round and round the garden with his arms stretched out. Vrrooom … he'd go. Vroom vrrooooom! The dog would wheeze and grin, his long tongue lolling.

Mrs Shambo would spot them through the kitchen window and rush out, waving a broomstick. Blackie would run off down the road, and Mrs Shambo would scold and shove the hero back into the house.

But towards the end of the winter vacation, things changed. Mrs Shambo suddenly fell ill and was taken away in an ambulance.

'Fantastic!' Situ exclaimed from behind the banyan tree. 'That old witch was so nasty to the poor Colonel. Now he can play with Blackie as much as he likes!'

But the old man went quiet instead. He did not act like a soldier anymore. While he fed Blackie, he'd keep mumbling into his headphones. Thangi and Situ-Gitu crept into his yard one day and hid behind a bush to listen. The colonel's words were very strange:

'Calling control room! Come in, control room! We have a problem. The sky has fallen to the ground and gotten all mucky! My aircraft is stuck!'

'What's he saying?' Thangi asked her friends, puzzled.

'Maybe he's hungry,' Gitu said timidly. 'What will he eat now that Mrs Shambo's gone?'

'What's it to you?' Situ asked nonchalantly. 'You can't cook anyway!'

When Thangi went home, her mother told her that the ladies in Chikku Colony were taking turns to send food for the colonel. It was their turn tomorrow.

'Amma, can I take the food over to him?' Thangi asked excitedly.

Her mother frowned. 'I don't know if you should. They say he's become a bit strange after the last war.'

'I'll take Situ-Gitu along,' Thangi said promptly. Amma sighed, and agreed.

Situ was in bed with a cold the next day. So Thangi and Gitu took food to the old man. Amma had prepared vegetable pulao for Colonel Shambo's lunch. Thangi knocked at the door, but nobody answered. They went around the house and peeped through the dirty windows, but couldn't see anyone inside.

'Maybe he's gone to visit Mrs Shambo at the hospital?' Gitu suggested. 'Let's go home.'

'We can't go back without checking on him properly,' Thangi said. 'Colonel Shambo might be in trouble. He might need rescuing! Remember what he was saying into the headphones?'

Gitu nodded uncertainly.

'What are we waiting for, then?' Thangi asked.

She struck a pose at the front door. 'HEEE-YAH!' She let fly her best karate kick. *Dham*! The unlocked door flew open and she landed hard on her bottom.

The dim, musty house was really quiet. Nothing was out of place except for an empty dagger-holder that lay on the floor. Gitu pointed at it and shivered. They walked into the dining room. A white bedsheet had been tied across four chairs. A tuneless whistle floated out from under it. Gitu stopped by the door, scared and ready to run.

Thangi's heart was pounding. The winter vacation had been boring this far, she thought. But not anymore. Here was fizz! She tiptoed up and placed the pot of rice on the table. Then she bent slowly and peeped under the tent. Colonel Shambo was there. He was pretending to make tea in a beaten-up teapot. The dagger was lying next to him. He'd cut a tomato with it. Its red juice made a small puddle on the floor.

When the colonel noticed Thangi, his eyes bulged horribly. 'The enemy attacks!' he shouted. Thangi jumped back, and Gitu ran away with a howl.

Suddenly he dropped his grey head and began to whimper, 'I want my Mala!'

Thangi had never seen a grown-up act like a child before. She felt sorry for him, but was really too scared to go close.

'The sky is dark and my plane is all mucky,' he wept.

Thangi sat on her haunches and watched him. He didn't look that different from Ajja, her grandfather who lived in Mysore. She took his hand and made him sit at the table. She served him vegetable pulao in a plate she found in the kitchen. She spilt it all over the place while serving it, but Colonel Shambo didn't mind at all. He just ate like he hadn't eaten in a long time.

That evening, Thangi sat on her swing and thought hard. She wanted to find a way to make Colonel Shambo happy. Just as the daylight began to fade, Thangi looked up. Her eyes were shining with a new idea. She called across the garden wall to Situ-Gitu.

The next day, the children set off for Pandupur Market. They walked into the hardware store and came out with a heavy package. Then, since they'd run out of money, they walked tiredly home.

The next morning, Thangi explained her idea to the colonel. It took some time for him to understand what she was proposing, but soon he was as excited as the rest. He gave the plan a thumbs up, pilot-style!

First, the children spread the white bedsheet (that Colonel Shambo had been using as a tent) across the front porch. While they were doing this, Blackie came to investigate. He sniffed around the big package, then ripped it open. 'Hey! See what Blackie's doing!' Situ shouted. Just as the dog raised his leg at the tins of paint and big brushes, the children shooed him away.

They got to work on the sheet. Colonel Shambo drew a beautiful aeroplane, like the one he had flown in the war. They painted it grey and silver. Then they made, in large sweeping strokes, a sky with fluffy white clouds at the top. The colonel painted a message at the bottom of the sheet in his best handwriting. By the end of it, the old man and the three children looked like bits of blue sky themselves.

Situ's mother tagged the sheet on a washing line. That night, Thangi dreamt that the stars had crowded around to admire it, wishing *their* sky was as pretty, and drying the paint with their sighs.

In the morning, the children helped Thangi's father hang the sheet over the outer wall of Colonel Shambo's house. The sheet covered the entire wall to the left of the front door. The silver paint sparkled in the sun.

Before long, a taxi drew up outside No. 37, with Mrs Shambo in it. She looked tired, but then her mouth dropped open at what she saw.

No. 37 had a sky blue face again! White clouds danced near the roof. Mrs Shambo leaned against the nurse's arm and stared at the beautiful silver-grey airplane. Her eyes shone, for in the pilot's seat was a hero. Colonel Shambo, in his army pilot uniform (that Gitu's mother had neatly pressed), was waving to his wife through a hole cut out in the sheet.

'WELCOME HOME DEAR MALA!' read the message he had painted.

Mrs Mala Shambo was helped to the door, and there, the colonel took her arm. He said "Vroooooom!" and this time, she laughed.

'We must have a party this very evening!' she exclaimed, the tiredness wiped off her face, 'with the sky blue sheet as a backdrop.'

It was a noisy party that followed. A host of grown-ups and children ate cake, mini-appams and chips, and danced madly to the latest pop songs. The clock struck five.

Thangi and Colonel Shambo were setting chairs out for the next game—musical chairs—when the winter sky turned the exact shade of blue as the bedsheet they'd painted. They stopped to stare as the thick clouds were whipped by an unexpected wind into rushing white ones with foamy edges. For an instant, the sky above house No. 37 became the faraway Himalayan one that Hero Shambo so loved.

When the sky returned to its regular colour, the colonel had tears on his wrinkly cheeks. Standing beside him was Mrs Shambo, her face wreathed in smiles. She hugged him tightly.

'Colonel Shambo is a hero again!' Thangi exclaimed.

'Mrs Shambo's hero!' giggled Gitu.

Situ turned cartwheels, and Blackie agreed with a bark.

5

MALLIPOO, FREE …

Adithi Rao

Nanja found Mallipoo sitting close to her mother's body, her leathery face stained with tears. Nanja approached slowly, not wanting to startle her. When he was just a few feet away, Mallipoo noticed him. He stopped and held out a hand.

'*Ba* ...' he whispered softly, 'come.'

The baby elephant looked at him in silence and turned away. So Nanja quietly went home.

The next morning, he returned to find her in the same place, her head resting close to her mother's still one, looking at her mother out of the corner of her eye. Nanja had brought a bunch of bananas from his orchard. He held one out to Mallipoo, but again she ignored him.

'I'll leave them here in case she gets hungry, and come back later,' thought Nanja. He left to collect wood for the evening fire.

Nanja had no luck with Mallipoo for two whole days. Each day on his way to work and on the way back he stopped to talk to her, offer her food and water. But she wouldn't even look at him. Then, on the third day, she suddenly raised her head and slowly extended her trunk and sniffed his hand. Nanja felt her soft breath blowing on his palm. After a while she got to her feet and followed him. A little distance ahead, she stopped and turned one last time to look at her mother, as if to say goodbye.

***

When Chella saw a baby elephant walking home beside her husband, she was surprised.

'Minchu! Savi!' she called excitedly. 'Come quickly!'

The children came running out into the garden and stopped in amazement. The three stepped back when Nanja and Mallipoo entered the little wooden gate. Savi moved nervously to stand behind her mother, but Minchu approached the baby elephant boldly. Mallipoo shied away.

'Not so soon, Minchu,' said Nanja. 'She's never been among humans before.'

That night, Nanja fed Mallipoo bananas and left her to sleep in the grain shed. When the place was still, Minchu crept out of the house, the kerosene lamp burning low in his hand. Mallipoo watched Minchu warily when he entered the shed, but he didn't go near her. He piled up some hay in the far corner, lay down on it and went to sleep. After a few minutes, lonely, sad little Mallipoo began to feel comforted by his presence. She put her head down on the red earth, and for the first time in three days, she slept.

Months passed. Mallipoo became part of Nanja's household and grew bigger by the day. Nanja stopped selling the bananas from his orchard.

'How can you keep giving them all away to the elephant? What will you live on if you don't sell them?' asked the neighbours. Nanja only smiled and shrugged.

Mallipoo seemed to understand the kindness she received in Nanja's home. One morning, when Chella came out of the house struggling with a pot of water, Mallipoo lifted it right out of her arms! Putting it onto her own back, she turned to Chella as if to say, 'Let's go, what are you waiting for?'

Surprised and touched, Chella laughed and led the way to the orchard, where the fruit trees had to be watered. It usually took many tiring trips between the well and the orchard, but today was different. Mallipoo carried the pots as if they weighed nothing, and the job was done in no time at all!

One day, Mallipoo disappeared for many hours. Just when Minchu set out to look for her, the family saw the elephant sauntering along the muddy path that led up from the forest. There was a large bundle of firewood on her back. From that day on, Nanja didn't have to go out to gather wood. It became Mallipoo's special task, and she took it very seriously.

Summer came to Pandupur, and with it came festivities and merrymaking. It was the time of the annual village fair. People from far and wide came to eat the delicious savouries fried in simmering pans of oil, to watch artists walk the tightrope, and buy the colourful toys on display. Savi was very excited. She was to meet her school friends Thangi, Situ and Gitu there. She couldn't wait! After much impatience and nagging, she finally dragged her laughing parents out of the house and away to the fair! Minchu was to water the fruit trees and follow later.

When Minchu entered the orchard, he stopped dead in horror. Two wild elephants had come in from the forest and broken into the neighbour's garden. Having ravaged in their search for food, they were now headed straight for Nanja's orchard!

'I must do something,' thought Minchu frantically, 'or they'll destroy everything!'

By now the elephants had reached the little wooden gate. With one heavy step, they smashed it to bits. Desperate, Minchu threw down the pot of water and ran back into the house. He grabbed a large iron vessel and a thick metal spoon and charged outside. He banged the spoon against the vessel again and again, hoping that the din would scare the wild elephants away.

It didn't.

Angered by the noise, the largest of the elephants stopped in the middle of uprooting a banana tree. It turned its head and fixed its cold eyes on Minchu. The hand that was beating the iron vessel froze mid-air. The elephant began to walk towards the boy, shaking its head, swinging its great trunk menacingly. Minchu was paralysed with fear …

***

At the fair, some of the villagers had climbed aboard the massive giant wheel.

'Appa, we want to get on too!' pleaded Savi, and Nanja swung her up into one of the cubicles. Gitu got in next to her, and Nanja helped Situ and Thangi into the cubicle behind. The ride started and the wheel began to turn, round and round, up and down, lifting the people high into the air and swooping them down towards the earth again. Savi and the others squealed in delight. They had never before ridden on a giant wheel as big as this one.

'It's such a funny feeling. When we go down, I feel as if my stomach follows a few seconds later … plop!' giggled Thangi.

The second time they reached the top, Gitu pointed into the distance delightedly. 'Look! On this side you can see the whole of Pandupur!'

'And on the other side,' Savi pointed, 'there's the river and the forest … and my home. My home!'

Down they went again. The third time they went up, Savi turned her head, hoping to catch a glimpse of Minchu outside the house.

She did. And she screamed.

***

The villagers panicked. They knew only too well the kind of damage a herd of wild elephants could cause. The lot of them ran towards Nanja's hut, armed with sticks and stones, beating large drums to scare off the elephants. Tears of terror were flowing down Chella's cheeks as she ran alongside Nanja.

The villagers reached Nanja's house and charged into the orchard. What they saw made them stop dead in their tracks. They were too late to save Minchu ... but only because Mallipoo had saved him first!

For there was Minchu facing the terrible wild elephants. And in-between them stood Mallipoo. No more was she the gentle baby Nanja had rescued from the forest. She suddenly looked big and very, very angry. Trumpeting loudly, she stamped her feet. The wild elephants were caught off guard and took a few steps backwards. Then Mallipoo lowered her great head and charged at them. The wild elephants turned and ran away. Mallipoo chased them until they disappeared into the forest ...

Chella rushed to Minchu and hugged him tightly. The villagers stood around, dazed and speechless by what they had just witnessed. Minutes later, Mallipoo lumbered back home, looking tired and dusty. Nanja walked up to her and slowly reached out with trembling arms. He wrapped them around her trunk, burying his face against her. No words came to him. But when he raised his head, Mallipoo's leathery grey skin was wet with his tears.

***

The rains had come and gone. Soon winter would be here, and firewood must be stacked aplenty to keep the fires burning through the cold months. Mallipoo went out everyday and returned with a bundle on her back. Then one day she didn't come at her usual hour, and Chella grew anxious. It was evening, and there was still no sign of her. Chella's anxiety blossomed into fear. By the time Nanja got home, she was frantic!

'Minchu looked everywhere but couldn't find her. Where could she have gone?' cried Chella to her husband.

'I'll go look for her,' said Nanja, trying to hide his own panic.

Minchu came running out of the hut. 'Wait, Appa! I'll come with you.'

Holding their kerosene lamps high above their heads, Minchu and Nanja set off into the forest, calling out to Mallipoo. Hours later, they gave up the search and returned home.

The next day, Nanja went to meet the forest officer, Mr Ponappa.

'I'm looking for my elephant, sir,' he said. 'She went to the forest to collect wood last morning and still hasn't returned.'

'I have been expecting you,' replied Ponappa. He was a middle-aged man with thinning hair and kind eyes behind his round spectacles.

'Me, sir? But how do you know me?'

'Not you in particular, but the owner of the elephant that I saw yesterday.'

'Oh,' said Nanja, his heart filling with hope. 'Then you know where she is?'

'I'm afraid not. You see, some poachers came to these parts to hunt for tuskers. We got there in time to stop them, but there was some exchange of gunfire. In the midst of that I saw an elephant with a bundle of wood run away deep into the forest. It must have been scared off by the noise.'

'She wasn't hurt by the bullets, was she?' asked a terrified Nanja, clutching at Mr Ponappa's arm.

'I'm not sure.'

Nanja returned home with the news. The family was plunged in gloom.

Many, many months passed. Yet not a day went by without Chella gazing down the forest path, hoping to see Mallipoo coming home to them. At night Savi cried herself to sleep, and Minchu hardly ever smiled anymore. The villagers noticed that Nanja still hadn't begun selling the bananas from his orchard.

'But why not?' they asked. 'You don't need them for Mallipoo anymore.'

Nanja shook his head. 'It just doesn't feel right.'

He went back to his old task of collecting wood from the forest. Only, now he went there as much to search for Mallipoo as to look for firewood. One day, deep in the forest, as he bent to pick a fallen branch, he saw a movement amidst the greenery. It was an elephant.

Mallipoo!

The animal moved to pluck some leaves, and that's when Nanja saw her baby beside her! His heart filled with love. As he made to hurry out from behind the trees and go to Mallipoo, a thought suddenly stopped him.

'She has made a life for herself in the forest,' thought Nanja to himself. 'Why should she come back to carrying firewood and watering orchards? After all, she's an elephant. And elephants are free ...'

Nanja watched this child of his with his heart in his eyes. Then he turned and quietly slipped away. A little distance away he stopped to look at her and her baby one last time, as if to say goodbye ...

NISHA

Chatura Rao

Nisha swings on the carved wooden swing, higher and higher and higher. Her feet swish through the long grass whenever they come down, and every time she goes up into the air, she feels like she can touch the swooping branches of the Gulmohar tree.

One of the older girls at school once told her that her name Nisha meant "darkness". But Jeevan Uncle had said that it meant "bad luck". Nisha believed him. Her mother had died soon after she was born and her father had gone away. The woman she now called Ma was really her mother's sister. She had taken the little girl home and named her Nisha.

Every day Ma drops Nisha to Saraswati Vidyashala School at 7.30 in the morning, a whole hour before the other children get there. Then she takes the bus to Durga Hills, to the house with the high walls and the beautiful garden.

Nisha's mother is secretary to Mrs Hussain, the wife of the general manager of the Dhun River Dam project. Mrs Hussain designs the interiors of people's houses. Sometimes Nisha's mother even travels with Mrs Hussain to big cities on projects. Until last month, Nisha always stayed at her neighbour Deepa's place when her mother was away. Deepa used to be her best friend. But since last month, Nisha's mother had no place to leave her. Nisha feels guilty about this problem …

Today is Good Friday, a holiday for Nisha, so Ma has brought her to work with her. Two children live next door to the Hussains—Raghav and Tara. They often call out to each other and to their dog, Archie. Ma wishes Nisha could be more lively, like them. She used to be.

Nisha and her mother live in a ground floor flat in New Society, not too far from Durga Hill. Deepa lives one floor above. Deepa's mother is the Maths teacher at Saraswati Vidyashala. Her mother and father fight, and only her mother goes to work. Nisha does not like other people's houses, and is secretly relieved that she is not allowed to go to Deepa's anymore.

Nisha hums very, very softly to herself as she swings. She is a thief, a good one. Yesterday she pinched two pencils from Stella. Stella had once pushed Nisha off a chair in class, so she deserves it.

'Hello!' Mrs Hussain calls to her from the kitchen step. 'Come over here!'

Nisha is slow to stop the swing. She doesn't want to look at Mrs Hussain, who she thinks must be a stupid lady. Finally, when her mother calls to her in their native language to hurry over, Nisha walks slowly across. But she doesn't look up.

'Hello,' the lady says again. 'What is your name? Would you like to eat something?' But Nisha won't look at her.

One evening, some days ago, she'd gone upstairs to call Deepa to play. Deepa's baby sister had been crying in the crib. Nisha had gone over to rock her, when Deepa's father put his hand on her shoulder from behind.

'Want a sweet, Nisha?' he had asked.

Nisha had felt afraid of him because he had red eyes that kept staring at her. Deepa had told her that her father was like a big cat with sharp claws and eyes that could see you in the dark. But Nisha had been hungry, so she'd nodded.

'But first I will check you. I am a doctor,' Deepa's father had said. Nisha didn't dare to look about, but somehow she knew that nobody else was in the house. She felt nervous but hadn't been able to say anything. It was as if something was stuck in her throat. 'Perhaps Jeevan Uncle is really a doctor,' she had thought.

The house had been quiet, though she could hear cars from the street. Then that noise too had gone away. She could only hear Jeevan Uncle breathing. The baby had stopped crying. Or maybe Nisha did not hear her anymore.

She felt dirty, but this was her fault. Why had she come into the house when Deepa was out?

Then he had said, 'This is our secret. Don't tell anybody about it. Here, take this sweet. There are more for you to eat if you come and play with me again.' Nisha took the sweet and darted past him. On a table by the door was a bottle half-filled with some drink. Nisha was a good thief—she had picked it up as she ran past him, and he had not noticed.

When Nisha got home that day, Ma was still out buying vegetables in the market. She had gone into her room and shut the door tightly. She had sat in a corner of her room and opened the bottle, put her mouth to it and taken a small lick. The drink had burnt her tongue and tasted horrible. As it is, she felt like throwing up. She had crept out into the street, and when no one was about, opened the cover and poured the drink into the gutter. She had hurled the sweet he had given her at his window on the first floor. Then she had thrown the bottle at the wall. It had crashed and broken into a thousand pieces. As she ran away, she heard Jeevan Uncle yell from the balcony after her.

Two days later, everybody found out about Jeevan Uncle and Nisha. This is how.

Ma had had to go in to work at six in the morning. She and Mrs Hussain were to take a train to Mysore to attend a meeting, and return to Pandupur the same evening. Ma had told Nisha to brush her teeth and make herself ready for school. Ma's friend Manisha would drop Nisha to school on her way to work.

Nisha had been sleeping when Ma left. But she had woken up suddenly and it was dark in the room. There was a shadow at the door.

'Don't be afraid,' the shadow said in a voice like dry leaves. 'It is just the doctor.'

She had sat up and clutched her sheet tightly. She could not say a word. Jeevan Uncle had come in and sat next to her on the bed.

'My angry little Nisha,' Jeevan Uncle had smiled and reached to touch her face. It was as if Nisha had turned to stone. Just then the door creaked open.

'Nisha?' Manisha Aunty's voice called. 'Who is here with you? Jeevan Kumar! What are you doing here?'

Nisha huddled into the sheet, hiding her face. She was trembling.

Manisha Aunty had taken Jeevan Uncle upstairs, and in a while Nisha could hear the grown-ups argue in loud voices. Deepa's mother had cried. Deepa never spoke to Nisha from that day on, except to say that she was a bad girl and everyone knew that now.

At home that night, Manisha Aunty had stayed for dinner. While cooking, Ma had wiped her eyes on her sleeve frequently. Nisha had felt cold and sad. Then Manisha Aunty had spoken softly in her ear, and Ma had nodded, but would not look up from the cooking.

'Come, Nisha, let's go for a walk,' Manisha Aunty said. Nisha got up and followed her. They went down the wide road between the buildings of New Society to the main street and sat at the bus stop on a bench. Nisha remembered that the moon had been large and silver. It was beautiful out there, except that it was night, and she was afraid of dark shadows and people who came out of them.

'Listen to me carefully now, Nisha. If a person ever touches you in a way that makes you feel bad or uncomfortable,' Manisha Aunty had said, 'you must tell them to stop! Tell them loudly. Shout if you have to. Do not be silent. And don't do anything that you don't like, even if the grown-up person tells you to.'

Nisha had nodded, but could not tell her about how dirty she felt, so she said, 'Ma is ashamed of me. She is angry that I was bad.'

'Bad?' Manisha Aunty looked genuinely puzzled. 'How were *you* bad?'

'Bad to go to Deepa's house when she was not home. Stupid.'

'Not stupid, nor bad, Nisha. You simply went to play with your friend. What happened to you was not your fault at all!'

'Why was Ma crying then?' Nisha had asked.

'She was crying because,' and Manisha Aunty hugged Nisha tightly before going on, 'Jeevan Uncle had given you a bad touch and made you sad. Ma loves you more than anyone in the whole world.'

Nisha was silent then. She felt sleepy.

That night she dreamed that Jeevan Uncle had come to the room again. Only this time she shouted at him, 'No! Go away!'

Nisha woke up with a start. Ma gave her water to drink and held her close. Nisha lay there, listening to the crickets chirp in the trees and bushes outside. Ma didn't often put an arm around her, but Nisha liked it when she did.

Now Nisha swings on the small wooden swing in Mrs Hussain's backyard. Then her mother gives her a mat so that she can lie on her stomach in the grass and look at the insects. She plays with stones and twigs, giving the twigs the names of her school friends. The stones she makes into her teachers.

Then it is time to go home. Ma calls her to the kitchen door. Mrs Hussain is there too, a cup of hot coffee in her hand. 'You didn't tell me your name,' she says. Nisha doesn't feel like saying it. Her name is bad luck. She keeps looking down.

'Nisha,' her mother says softly. She sounds as if she is smiling as she says it. Perhaps she has always said it in this way, only, Nisha never noticed before.

'What a lovely name,' Mrs Hussain says. 'Night.'

Ma nods.

'So your name,' Mrs Hussain says, gently lifting Nisha's chin, 'belongs to the night, to peace and rest, to the stars, the silver moon and owls.'

Nisha raises her eyes to meet Mrs Hussian's eyes, brown like coffee. She looks past her and sees the house where her mother spends her whole day. It has books, colourful curtains, paintings and photographs of the lady's family.

On the way back home, Ma holds Nisha's hand on the bus, and sometimes she smiles out of the window. Nisha thinks about what her name really means and doesn't feel much like she's bad luck or darkness anymore.

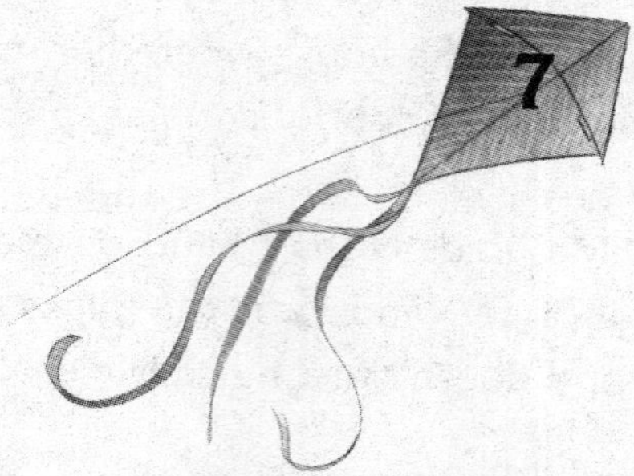

7

ABOUT GRANDFATHERS AND TREES

Adithi Rao

At 5 feet 4 inches, my Ajja is the tallest man in the world. He's plump and cuddly, has laughing eyes, bright silver hair and big funny ears. He can waggle his ears without touching them, just by wiggling his eyebrows, and he can stick out his tongue and touch the tip of his nose. In case you think that's easy, you should try doing it sometime. Go on, try it ... See how hard it is? Don't worry, I can't do it either, and I really tried, believe me! I tried till my jaws ached and my nose nearly fell off. It still didn't work.

Here's another thing about my Ajja. He hasn't told anybody else but me, and I'm telling you now. Just remember, though, it's a secret. Anyway, if you told a grown-up person, they wouldn't believe you. So here's the secret. My Ajja is a magician. He was born in Burma, and worked as a doctor there. During that time he only returned once to India to marry Ammama, my grandmother, and take her back with him. But after my mother was born, Ajja retired and left Burma forever. He returned to live in Chikku Colony, in his hometown of Pandupur. He brought his wife and little daughter with him. He also brought back the magic of *Oompha! Pyausay!*

Ajja continued to work as a doctor in Pandupur, and everybody in the town loved him dearly. Doctors, as you know, are people who hand out medicines and bandage up bruised knees, cut open people and sew them back together. Except that my Ajja doesn't need to do any of those things. He can just pass his hand over a sick person, over the part where it hurts, and they become alright immediately!

Once Checha pushed me when we were playing running-and-catching, and I fell and had a big wound on my leg. All our friends gathered around, and there was so much blood that they began to scream. That scared me and I started screaming too. Some of the bigger ones, Situ and Thangi and Ranjani, carried me into the house to Ajja. While they were all losing their heads and Ammama was crying, Ajja took me by the shoulders till I came around. Then he said very quietly so that nobody else would hear, 'Do you trust me?'

I nodded.

'Then I can make the pain go away.'

He passed his hand over my bruised and bleeding knee. He muttered the words, '*Oompha*! *Pyausay*!'

For a second, all the shouting and crying noises in the background faded away. It was as if I was sitting inside a seashell and I could hear them all, but from a great distance away. The next second the stinging in my leg disappeared, and I felt cool and tingly and calm all over. When I drifted back, I blinked and looked down. There was not a scratch to be seen, and Ajja was quickly binding up my knee. *Oompha*! *Pyausay*! I remember my grandmother telling me once long ago that these were Burmese healing words ...

'You're a magician!' I whispered in wonder.

Ajja looked up from what he was doing. His face was very solemn, but his eyes were twinkling. I knew I was right!

'But why are you bandaging my leg?' I whispered again.

'Because.' he replied simply, and shrugged.

I understood. He didn't want anyone else to see that he had healed my leg with magic. I must be the only one to know. Just me and Ajja. And now you.

That wasn't the only sort of magic my grandfather could do. Once at the railway station, when he came to put my mother and me back on the train to Madras at the end of the summer vacation, there was a lady with a small baby waiting to board the same train. Her baby was fretting and crying. She tried cuddling and patting, feeding and singing, but it only cried harder. Pretty soon everybody on the platform was looking around to see what the commotion was about. A little way off, a man with a briefcase looked up from his book in irritation. One woman left her group and came over to the mother to give her some helpful advice that didn't help at all. Soon people lost interest and went back to their business.

Ajja let go of my hand and casually strolled across to the newspaper stand, close to where the mother and her baby were. He picked up a copy of the *Pandupur Times* and paid for it. As he turned away, he looked directly at the screaming baby over the mother's shoulder, right into its teary brown eyes. The baby paused halfway through a yell. I saw Ajja whisper the words, '*Oompha*! *Pyousay*!' and wink.

The baby gave a small gurgle of surprise. Its tiny face, that had been yelling and oozing tears for nearly twenty minutes, suddenly split into a wet, toothless smile!

Ajja rejoined us and I looked up at him, grinning delightedly. He avoided my eyes, opened his newspaper and started to read. But I noticed the side of his mouth twitch for a moment. He *had* done it! My magician grandpa had made the baby stop crying. I didn't care that he didn't tell me; I *knew*!

The next summer I returned to Pandupur as usual. There was a bumper crop of mangoes that year and everybody ate and ate till they started to look like fruit flies. My Ajja and I were the only ones who didn't eat too many. Ajja preferred bananas, and I only like mangoes that are sweet and sour, not one or the other. One day, after my mother and grandmother finished lunch and started on the mangoes, I happened to pick up a *raspuri*, a particular variety of the fruit that was just perfect. Not too sweet, not too sour, amber-coloured and juicy. So I ate it. Then I gnawed on the seed until it was quite bald.

'Why don't you plant it?' suggested Ajja.

'I can do that?' I asked, wide-eyed.

'Why not? There is a free patch in the garden. Just dig up the earth, put it in and cover it up. If we water it every day, we'll probably have a mango tree in no time.'

'You should,' urged Ammama, her mouth full of mango. 'Your Ajja will look after it for you when you are away at school. I don't know how he does it, but most things he plants start to bear fruit in a year. It's some kind of fertilizer he uses, I think.'

'Ma,' sighed my mother in exasperation, 'how can that possibly be? No tree will give fruit in a year. Not unless you use magic!' She apparently found this last thought of hers quite funny because she was still chuckling when Ajja and I left the room.

Outside, we got the spade and dug a hole. I will never forget that day, working quietly out in the back garden with my grandfather, my fingernails stained with the red Pandupur soil, the sun warm on our backs. When I got it right, he nodded at me and smiled. He always smiled with his eyes. His smile is another reason I remember that day. That, and because it was my last summer with him.

Eleven months later, back in Madras, the telephone rang. It was just after dinner and the family was gathered around the television set. Ma hurried to the next room to pick up the phone. I heard her speak for a moment and then she gave a cry. My father rushed to her and there was a flurry of voices. When they returned to the living room, my mother was crying bitterly and my father's arm was around her. He looked upset too.

'You leave by the early morning train. I'll arrange for leave from work and from Avi's school, and bring him later tomorrow. Anyway, he doesn't need to see ... well, you know.'

My mother nodded and they went off to pack her bag.

I don't really know how I was feeling at that moment. Looking back, I think I wasn't feeling anything at all. Ma left in the morning, Papa made all the arrangements, locked up the house and took me with him to the Madras Central station. By the time we stepped off the train in Pandupur, it was 3 o'clock in the afternoon, the day after the phone call had come. I automatically looked up and down the station platform out of habit, expecting to see my grandfather waiting for me with his cheery smile and his arms wide open. Instead, my father and I made our way outside and took a rickshaw.

When we reached the old brown cottage in Chikku Colony, it looked as serene as ever. The flowers in the front garden were in full bloom, as if the magician who looked after them was sitting in the next room. Only, this time my grandmother wasn't waiting for me in the veranda as she usually did. This time I had to go inside to her.

The house looked freshly scrubbed. My mother and grandmother and some other people were sitting around in the drawing room. They looked sad. Ammama clung to me when she saw me. She had no tears in her eyes, but I could tell that her heart was crying.

A little while later, I felt that the lump in my throat was getting too tight to bear. So I got up and wandered off by myself. In my seven years I had never seen the house messy, or anything out of place. Today was no different. I went into Ajja's room. I was afraid it would make me cry, but it didn't. His bed was neatly made and his clothes were hung up on the clothes stand just as always. I sat on the bed for a while and then leaned forward and buried my face in his pillow. It smelled of him, and the sheets smelled of cotton and summertime and all the things that made me happy. I got up, crossed over to his cupboard and opened it. His wallet was there, his watch, his comb, his stethoscope (one of those things doctors put in their ears to listen to people's heartbeats). I found an old black-and-white photo of his mother, whom he had loved dearly. Then I found an envelope with my name on it.

Curiously, I reached out and picked it up and returned to sit on the bed. Inside, there was a letter. It said:

Dear Avi,

I never told you this before, but you're a magician too. You don't know it yet, but as time goes on, you'll see. Now all you have to do is believe it. It is something I have given to you. You will do many wonderful things with your gift, I know, and I can think of nobody better to pass on this special power of mine to. Use it well. Someday you'll be an even better magician than I ever was.

Love,

Ajja

Clutching the letter close to my chest, I began to pace the room. My heart was singing. Suddenly I felt like my grandfather had come back to me. He had come to live inside me!

The next morning I woke to the sound of birds chirping happily in the backyard. Suddenly I remembered something I had forgotten to check the previous day. I jumped out of bed, ran through the house and out the back door into the garden where Ajja and I had planted the mango seed the previous summer. Ammama was right. It was full of mangoes! I stood under it and looked up into its branches above.

It was the tallest tree in the world.